STARTING OUT

baby ORANGUTANS

KATE RIGGS

CREATIVE EDUCATION • CREATIVE PAPERBACKS

CONT

ENTS

I AM AN INFANT.

I am a baby orangutan.

Look at my red hair and long arms!

I weighed about three pounds (1.4 kg) at birth.

I will drink my mother's milk until I am four or five.

My mother and I live in the trees. We swing from branch to branch.

Every night, we
make a new nest.

I start eating plants and fruits. I am called a juvenile.

Now I am a young orangutan!

SPEAK AND LISTEN

WOOO!

Can you speak like an infant? Orangutans rumble, howl, squeak, and call.

Listen to these sounds:

https://wildambience.com/wildlife-sounds/orangutan/

Now it is your turn!

INFANT WORDS

branch: a part of a tree that grows out of the trunk

juvenile: a young orangutan, between the ages of five and eight

READING CORNER

Kelley, K. C. *Baby Orangutans*. North Mankato, Minn.: Amicus, 2018.

Leaf, Christina. *Baby Orangutans*. Minneapolis: Bellwether Media, 2015.

Storm, Marysa. *Orangutans*. North Mankato, Minn.: Black Rabbit Books, 2020.

INDEX

PUBLISHED BY CREATIVE EDUCATION AND CREATIVE PAPERBACKS
P.O. Box 227, Mankato, Minnesota 56002
Creative Education and Creative Paperbacks are imprints of The Creative Company
www.thecreativecompany.us

LIBRARY OF CONGRESS CATALOGING-IN-PUBLICATION DATA
Names: Riggs, Kate, author.
Title: Baby orangutans / Kate Riggs.
Series: Starting out.
Summary: A baby orangutan narrates the story of its life, describing how physical features, diet, habitat, and familial relationships play a role in its growth and development.

Identifiers: ISBN 978-1-64026-351-2 (hardcover)
ISBN 978-1-62832-883-7 (pbk)
ISBN 978-1-64000-493-1 (eBook)
This title has been submitted for CIP processing under LCCN 2020901903.

CCSS: RI.K.1, 2, 3, 4, 5, 6, 7; RI.1.1, 2, 3, 4, 5, 6, 7; RF.K.1, 3; RF.1.1

DESIGN AND PRODUCTION
by Chelsey Luther and Joe Kahnke
Art direction by Rita Marshall
Printed in China

PHOTOGRAPHS by Alamy (Nature Picture Library, Ian Wood), Dreamstime (Isselee), Getty Images (Dimas Ardian/Stringer), Minden Pictures (Suzi Eszterhas, Anup Shah), Shutterstock (Bohbeh, Eric Isselee, panpilai paipa, WayneImage)

FIRST EDITION HC 9 8 7 6 5 4 3 2 1
FIRST EDITION PBK 9 8 7 6 5 4 3 2 1